IT'S NO BIG DILL!

This book belongs to:

_____

Visit us on the Web! rhcbooks.com

Educators and librarians, for a variety of teaching tools, visit us at RHTeachersLibrarians.com

Library of Congress Cataloging-in-Publication Data

Names: Holt, Bob, author, illustrator.

Title: Let's taco about how great you are / by Bob Holt.

Description: First edition. | New York : Doubleday, [2021] | Audience: Ages 4–8. | Summary: "A food-themed,

pun-filled book of advice and encouragement for children" —Provided by publisher.

Identifiers: LCCN 2020010051 (print) | LCCN 2020010052 (ebook)

ISBN 978-0-593-18201-7 (hardcover) | ISBN 978-0-593-18202-4 (library binding) | ISBN 978-0-593-18203-1 (ebook)

Subjects: CYAC: Encouragement—Fiction. | Food—Fiction. | Humorous stories.

Classification: LCC PZ7.1.H6468 Let 2020 (print) | LCC PZ7.1.H6468 (ebook) | DDC [E]—dc23

MANUFACTURED IN CHINA   10 9 8 7 6 5 4 3 2 1   First Edition

Let's Taco ABOUT HOW GREAT YOU ARE

Bob Holt

Doubleday Books for Young Readers

HOT
DIGGITY
DOG

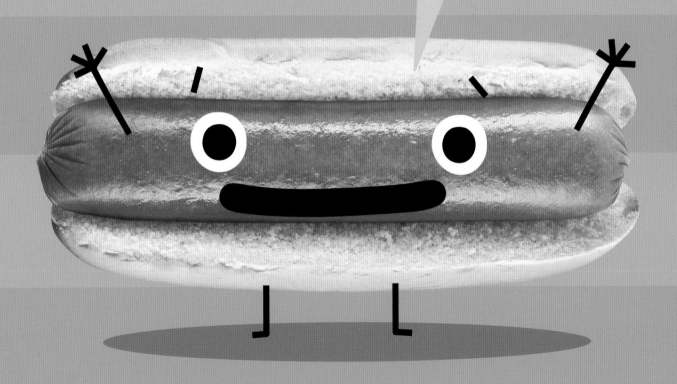

SOOOOOOO
HaP-

-Pea

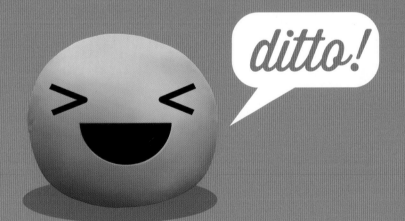

ditto!

To Know ya!

YOU GUAC MY WORLD!

YOU'RE a SMaRTY PaNTS

DONUT
KNOW HOW YOU
DO IT ...

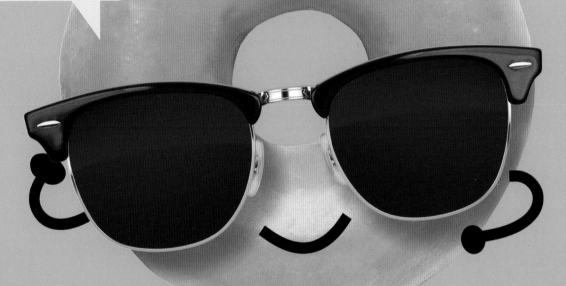

REMEMBER, NOT EVERY DAY WILL BE GRAPE

Monday

Tuesday

Wednesday

Thursday

Friday

Saturday

Yep

Some days
are lemons

Sunday

THINGS WON'T ALWAYS GO YOUR WAY. YOU CAN BACON THAT!

Lemme give you a few
ASPARAGUS
TIPS

Don't Let Life

wheee!

PASTA YOU BY

LIFE is GOUDA

ALWayS FinD a
Raisin

TO
SMILE!

SHOULD YOU WORRY?

NOBODY KNOWS BUTTER THAN YOU

conquering LIFe'S CHaLLenges can make you FeeL Like...

IT'S BECOME apPEARent

so
Lettuce
all
Yell...

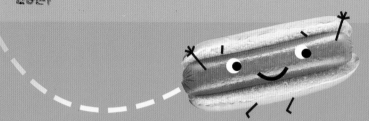